Annika Riz, Math Whiz

Also by

Claudia Mills

Dinah Forever

Losers, Inc.

Standing Up to Mr. O.

You're a Brave Man, Julius Zimmerman

Lizzie at Last

7 × 9 = Trouble!

Alex Ryan, Stop That!

Perfectly Chelsea

Makeovers by Marcia

Trading Places

Being Teddy Roosevelt

The Totally Made-up Civil War Diary of Amanda MacLeish

How Oliver Olson Changed the World

One Square Inch

Fractions = Trouble!

Kelsey Green, Reading Queen

Zero Tolerance

Franklin School Friends

Annika Riz, Math Whiz

Claudia Mills

pictures by Rob Shepperson

Margaret Ferguson Books
Farrar Straus Giroux • New York

Farrar Straus Giroux Books for Young Readers
175 Fifth Avenue, New York 10010

Designed by Elizabeth H. Clark
Printed in the United States of America by
RR Donnelley & Sons Company, Harrisonburg, Virginia
First edition, 2014
3 5 7 9 10 8 6 4 2

mackids.com

Library of Congress Cataloging-in-Publication Data
Mills, Claudia.
Annika Riz, math whiz / Claudia Mills ; pictures by Rob Shepperson. — First edition.
pages cm
Summary: Annika hopes to change her best friends' hatred of math by winning a Sudoku contest, but she does not realize how important their lack of mathematical ability is until they make a mistake at the school carnival.
ISBN 978-0-374-30335-8 (hardcover)
ISBN 978-0-374-30336-5 (ebook)
[1. Mathematics—Fiction. 2. Schools—Fiction. 3. Contests—Fiction. 4. Carnivals—Fiction. 5. Friendship—Fiction.] I. Shepperson, Rob, illustrator. II. Title.

PZ7.M63963Ann 2014
[Fic]—dc23

2013012328

Farrar Straus Giroux Books for Young Readers may be purchased for business or promotional use. For information on bulk purchases please contact Macmillan Corporate and Premium Sales Department at (800) 221-7945 x5442 or by email at specialmarkets@macmillan.com.

To Cheryl Mills, math whiz and wonderful sister
—C.M.

For Semarya
—R.S.

Annika Riz, Math Whiz

1

Annika Riz sharpened her already sharp pencil. She admired its soft pink eraser. She never made mistakes during math—well, hardly ever—but it was good to have a pencil with a fresh eraser just in case. In five minutes—no, four and a half minutes now—it would be her favorite time of the day, which happened to be the least favorite time of the day for her two best friends, Kelsey Green and Izzy Barr.

Math!

"All right, class, time for math!" Mrs. Molina told her third graders.

Sitting in front of Annika, Kelsey gave a deep sigh and tried to finish reading one more page of her library book. Sitting next to Kelsey, Izzy sighed, too. She had been staring out the window at the P.E. field, green on this first Monday morning of May.

Kelsey loved reading and Izzy loved running the same way that Annika loved math. But Annika didn't hate reading and running the same way that the others hated math. It was hard when your two best friends hated the thing that you loved the most in the world.

At his perfectly tidy desk, Simon Ellis sat with his math book open, ready to go. Simon was a math whiz, too. Simon was an everything whiz.

The only person without a math book on top of his desk was Cody Harmon. Cody hardly ever paid attention in class.

As Mrs. Molina prepared to launch into the day's math lesson, her gaze fell on Cody.

"Math time, Cody," she said.

Yes, Annika thought. *Math time, everybody!*

When Cody still didn't take out his book, Mrs. Molina asked, "What is it, Cody?"

She sounded impatient, as if she really wanted to ask, "What is it *now*?" Annika didn't blame her. Every day there was someone who was reading during math time (Kelsey), or stretching her leg muscles during math time (Izzy), or doing nothing at all during math time (Cody).

"I heard there's going to be a dunking tank at the carnival on Saturday," Cody said. "And that people can buy tickets to dunk Mr. Boone."

Now the classroom was abuzz. Everyone obviously thought a dunking tank at the upcoming Franklin School carnival was more exciting than learning about decimals. Especially if it was the jolly principal, Mr. Boone, who was volunteering to be dunked.

"That's nice, Cody," Mrs. Molina said,

MATH
MATH

although it was plain from the expression on her face that she didn't think a dunking tank was nice at all.

"I heard that some of the teachers are signing up to be dunked, too," Cody continued.

Mrs. Molina adjusted her glasses, in the way she always did when she wasn't sure what to say. Annika knew that Mrs. Molina was the last teacher in the school—in the whole entire world—who would sign up to be dunked at a school carnival.

This time Mrs. Molina didn't say that was nice.

"The school carnival is always enjoyable, I'm sure," she said. "And it's the most important fund-raiser of the year for the PTA. But right now we're doing math. So, Cody, please get out your math book and open it to page 187."

Cody fumbled in his desk, dragged out his book, and opened it as instructed. Annika could tell that he was still thinking about the dunking tank, and probably also about cotton candy, and a fishpond where you could fish for prizes, and the raffle where the prize was an enormous stuffed elephant donated by a local toy store, already sitting in the front hall outside Mr. Boone's office.

Each class was going to have its own booth at the fair. Mrs. Molina's class booth, supervised by Kelsey's mom, who was their PTA room mother, was going to sell all different kinds of cookies. Annika, Kelsey, and Izzy had already decided that they would bake chocolate chip.

"Today we're going to learn how to turn fractions into decimals," Mrs. Molina said, obviously relieved to have diverted the conversation away from dunking tanks.

Annika listened eagerly as Mrs. Molina explained how decimals were another way of expressing fractions. She already loved fractions, and now she knew she'd love decimals, too.

As usual, Mrs. Molina called on people to give answers to the problems in the textbook. She probably did it so that people wouldn't tune out completely, knowing that there was some chance of being called on and having to give a wrong answer in front of the whole class.

Annika answered her question, easy-peasy, and Simon answered his, too. But then Mrs. Molina called on Kelsey.

"Kelsey Green"—Mrs. Molina used a person's full name if she was certain the person wasn't paying attention at all—"what decimal is one-third?"

Sitting directly behind Kelsey, Annika whispered the answer. Even though Kelsey should have been doing her own work, Annika couldn't bear to see her friends flounder. And she couldn't bear to leave a math question unanswered, any more than she could bear to leave a blank space in a sudoku puzzle.

"Point three three three."

"Point three three three," Kelsey parroted.

Mrs. Molina gave her a suspicious look, but Annika had gotten so good at whispering without moving her lips that they hadn't gotten caught once all year. Of course, the teacher had to notice that certain of her students who did well in class did vastly less well on their tests. But, then again, math tests made lots of people nervous.

When it came time for the class to do some problems quietly on their own, Annika finished hers in a few minutes. Then she tiptoed over to the pile of sudoku puzzles and word searches Mrs. Molina kept on her desk for kids who finished an assignment early. She took a sudoku puzzle from the top of the pile and returned to her seat.

Sudoku puzzles were tons of fun. You started with a nine-by-nine grid that had some numbers already filled in and others left blank. You had to fill in the blank spaces so that each row contained all the numbers from 1 to 9, and each column contained all the numbers from 1 to 9, and each little three-by-three box in the nine-by-nine grid had all the numbers from 1 to 9, too.

Right away, studying the puzzle in front of her, Annika saw where she could put a 9. And then where she could put a 5, and another 5. Her fingers flew over the page.

The other kids around her were still working on their decimal problems, but she could see that Simon was doing a sudoku puzzle, too.

"Annika, Simon, would you please come up here for a minute?" Mrs. Molina said.

Annika glanced toward Simon, but he seemed as bewildered as she was. It couldn't be that they were in trouble. Not during math! Not when they were the two math whizzes!

Mrs. Molina spoke in a low voice so as not to disturb the others.

"Because the two of you are our sudoku enthusiasts, I wanted to let you know that the public library is having a citywide sudoku contest this week. I received an e-mail about it this morning. Just go to the library any day, from today until the library's closing time on Saturday. Tell the librarian you want to enter the contest, and she'll sit you down with a sudoku puzzle. The person who completes the puzzle correctly in the shortest time wins. The winner for each grade will receive a subscription to a sudoku magazine."

Annika looked at Simon.

Simon looked at Annika.

Of course, third graders from all the elementary schools in town would be entering, too, and there might be another third grader at another elementary school who was even better at math than Annika and Simon.

Frankly, Annika found that hard to believe.

This was better than chocolate chip cookies, or cotton candy, or a fishpond with prizes, even better than a dunking tank with Mr. Boone poised to splash into the water beneath.

If Annika won a huge sudoku contest, Kelsey and Izzy would see that math was as cool as reading and running. Kelsey loved reading contests, and Izzy loved running races. Well, now Annika had a math contest and a math race of her own.

All she had to do was win it.

2

Kelsey and Izzy called Annika's house "the math house." Everyone in Annika's family was a math person. Her father was a high school math teacher who taught hard math classes like trigonometry and calculus. Her mother was a tax accountant who worked with numbers all day long. So Annika's house had all kinds of math things in it.

Bookcases filled with books about math.

Magnetic numerals arranged in equations on the refrigerator door.

Kitchen curtains with cheery blue and orange numerals printed all over them.

Even their salt and pepper shakers were shaped like numerals. Salt was shaped like a 3. Pepper was shaped like a 4. Annika sometimes wondered what was supposed to be especially salty about 3 and peppery about 4, but the two shakers did look cute side by side on the kitchen table.

Of course, once people knew you were a math family living in a math house, they started buying you math-themed holiday presents.

Ties with equations on them for her father.

Scarves with equations on them for her mother.

For Annika, a T-shirt with the most famous equation of all: $E = mc^2$. Annika's parents had told her it meant that energy equals mass times the speed of light squared. She didn't know exactly what all those things were, but she knew that Albert Einstein had discovered the equation, and that it was the most famous equation in the history of the world. She felt smart whenever she wore that T-shirt.

She'd wear the $E = mc^2$ T-shirt when she did the sudoku contest.

Annika's father drove her home to their math house that afternoon from Kelsey's after he finished coaching the high school math team. Annika and Izzy usually went to Kelsey's house after school, because Kelsey's mom was a stay-at-home mom, and all the other parents were still at work.

As soon as they reached the front door, Annika's brown-and-white beagle came running to greet her. The next thing she knew, he was jumping on her and barking a welcome; when she stooped down to hug him, he gave her a welcoming face-washing as well.

"Down, Prime! Sit, Prime!" Annika commanded. Given that she was already hugging him, he didn't pay any more attention to her scolding than most of her classmates had paid to Mrs. Molina's lecture about decimals.

Prime was short for Prime Number. Those were the most intriguing numbers of all, numbers that couldn't be divided by anything except for themselves and 1. Annika had a place mat printed with a list of prime numbers, starting with 1, 2, 3, 5, 7, 11, 13, 17, and 19, and going all the way up to 997.

Annika was trying to teach Prime to do math tricks. Though maybe she should have started with training him to sit, stay, and heel. He still jumped on everyone who came into the house, wagging his tail hard enough to raise a breeze.

While her father started to prepare supper, Annika gave Prime a math training session.

She wanted to teach him to count: to give one bark if he got one dog biscuit, two barks if he got two dog biscuits, three barks for three dog biscuits, and so on. For now, it would be enough if he could learn to count to three, even though she had seen a video of a dog on the Internet who could give the correct number of barks for questions like "What is two times three?" and "What is one plus four?"

In any case, right now Prime couldn't count at all.

Annika held up one dog biscuit.

He barked four times.

She held up two dog biscuits.

He barked three times.

How *did* you teach a dog to count?

"Prime," she said, trying to make her voice stern like Mrs. Molina's. "You are never going to learn any math if you don't pay attention. All right, Prime. This is *one* dog biscuit."

As she said the number loudly and clearly, she held the biscuit low enough for him to see, but high enough that he couldn't reach it. He jumped up to try to snatch it away.

"No, Prime. Sit! Listen, Prime. When you get *one* dog biscuit, you give *one* bark like this."

Annika gave her best imitation of a bark.

Over at the stove, sautéing chopped onions and mushrooms for spaghetti sauce, Annika's father chuckled.

Prime barked twice. Well, two was only one number away from the correct answer. Two barks were closer to one bark than four barks had been. Maybe they were making progress.

She knew she shouldn't reward Prime unless he got the answer right, but it seemed mean to make him wait any longer. So she let him grab the dog biscuit from her fingers.

"Good dog, Prime," she said. It was important to sound encouraging, or else her first and only pupil might give up on math entirely.

Annika waited to tell her father about the sudoku contest until her mother was home, too, and they were all sitting at the dinner table together.

First she told them what Cody had said about the carnival.

"Cody Harmon said there's going to be a dunking tank at the carnival and Mr. Boone is going to be dunked," she reported.

"That's another reason I'd never want to be a principal," her father said. "You'd always be getting dunked, or kissing a pig, or sitting on top of a flagpole."

Mr. Boone had never sat on top of a flagpole. But he *had* kissed a pig once.

"Besides," her father added, "if I were a principal, I couldn't be in the classroom doing what I love best, which is teaching math."

"Some of the teachers are getting dunked, too."

"Not Mrs. Molina, I bet," her father said.

"Do you blame her?" her mother asked. "That's one thing I don't have to worry about as a tax accountant. We're completely safe from dunking tanks, thank goodness."

"Would you let your students dunk *you*?" Annika asked her father.

"It wouldn't be my first choice as a way to spend an evening," he said. "But if everyone else was doing it, I'd try to be a good sport, I suppose."

Annika was sure that her father was a lot more fun as a teacher than Mrs. Molina. She didn't think he'd call on people who weren't paying attention in class and risk embarrassing them when they couldn't give the correct answer.

Still, she was grateful to Mrs. Molina for sharing news of the library sudoku contest with her and Simon.

"Guess what?" she asked both her parents then, laying down her fork.

Before they could offer any guesses, she went on. "Mrs. Molina told Simon and me about a contest the library is having. It's not a reading contest, it's a sudoku contest! And guess when it is? This week! There's going to be a winner for every grade."

"That's pretty exciting," her mother said.

Her father grinned and raised two thumbs up.

"I'm always doing sudoku puzzles anyway," Annika said, "but I want to do them faster. Can you teach me any tricks?"

Both her parents were great with math tricks. They should be the ones to work on teaching Prime to count, though so far they hadn't shown any interest in that project.

"After dinner we can do a few puzzles together from one of your sudoku books," her mother suggested.

"We'll see what we can come up with," her father agreed.

Maybe it was unfair to the other contestants that Annika got to live in a math house with math parents and a mathematically minded dog, or at least a dog with a mathematical name. Of course, she didn't know what kind of house Simon lived in. But he was awfully good at math anyway.

For luck, Annika sprinkled a little bit of salt on the rest of her spaghetti from the shaker shaped like a 3 and a little bit of pepper from the shaker shaped like a 4. If she was going to beat Simon Ellis at the sudoku contest, she might as well take advantage of all the help she could get.

3

During math time on Tuesday, it wasn't Cody who interrupted Mrs. Molina to talk about the carnival. It was Mr. Boone.

He came bounding into the room—principals didn't need to knock—just as Mrs. Molina was about to call on the boy who sat behind Cody and who paid almost as little attention as Cody did.

Mr. Boone was a big round jolly man who had once had a big full jolly beard that he shaved off to reward the Franklin School students for completing a school-wide reading contest earlier that spring. Now Kelsey called him Mr. Moon; he looked like the picture a kindergartner would draw of a beaming moon lighting up the night sky.

Mrs. Molina gave him a small chilly smile in return. Annika knew she thought it was bad enough when kids in the class wasted time during math, but at least then she could make them open their math books to page 187 or page 192 or whatever page she wanted. She couldn't do anything about Mr. Boone.

Today he was whistling circus-style music, as if he were heralding a parade of costumed elephants entering the big top.

That would be all Mrs. Molina would need: elephants in her room during math time! Annika suppressed a giggle, but the rest of the class was already laughing in relief at Mr. Boone's comic entrance.

"Who's ready for the carnival?" he called out.

"We are!" the class chorused back.

"Well, I'm not," he said, trying to make himself sound worried. "I've heard a terrible rumor that I may be getting very wet this Saturday between five and eight in the evening. But surely no one at this fine school would pay money to dunk *me*, right?"

The class roared with laughter.

"Of course we're not ready for the carnival quite yet," he said, turning serious. "There is still a lot to do. One fifth-grade class is renting a cotton candy machine. One second-grade class is selling popcorn. And one fourth-grade class is planning something extremely gross and disgusting for their booth."

"What is it?" several kids called out.

Mr. Boone grinned. "You'll have to come to the carnival to find out. I've also heard that your class is going to be selling the world's tastiest cookies. Is that right?"

"Yes!" all the kids shouted.

"So I've come in today, borrowing some of Mrs. Molina's valuable class time, to remind you to do your best baking."

He nodded appreciatively to Mrs. Molina, as if she had invited him into her class rather than having him barge in like a circus elephant himself.

Mr. Boone continued. "Even more, I want all of you to come to the carnival with your parents, siblings, uncles, aunts, grandparents, and neighbors, so we can make this Franklin School carnival the most successful carnival ever. Are you with me?"

The class cheered.

Then, renewing his circus whistle, Mr. Boone made his exit.

With the disappearance of Mr. Boone, the classroom seemed a good deal duller than it had a minute before.

"Jacob Evans," Mrs. Molina said, calling on the boy behind Cody, "what is the answer to problem seventeen?"

Annika took her sudoku book outside for lunch recess. She sat on a shady bench doing a puzzle while Kelsey sat next to her reading and Izzy joined a kickball game.

On the matching bench across the playground, Simon sat by himself, obviously working through a sudoku puzzle, too.

Annika pushed herself to complete her puzzle faster. She was going to have to start timing herself, using the stopwatch feature on the new wristwatch she had gotten for her birthday.

Finally she filled in the last box.

"Done!" she crowed.

She looked over at Simon, bent over his own sudoku book. Was he still working on the same puzzle, or had he already started on a new one?

She hadn't told her friends about the sudoku contest yet. She wanted to wait until the announcement came that she had won, that she was the best sudoku-puzzle-solver out of every single third grader in every single school in the entire city. Last night she had asked her father how many elementary schools there were in the district, and he had told her: eleven!

You beat every third grader in all eleven schools? Izzy and Kelsey would exclaim when they found out.

Yes, Annika would say, trying to look modest. And then she would add, *See what happens when you pay attention during math?* No, she wouldn't say that. She'd let them draw that conclusion themselves.

Gosh, Annika, we never knew you could win a really cool contest just by doing math! Kelsey would say.

Gee, Annika, maybe math is more important than we thought! Izzy would say.

Yes, she would tell them about the contest when she won.

If she won.

Kelsey had read her a story once about a milkmaid who was carrying home a pail of milk balanced on her head. The milkmaid was thinking about all the butter she could churn from the milk, and all the eggs she could buy from selling the butter, and all the chickens she could hatch from the eggs. She got so excited counting up all these chickens that she did a happy little jig, which caused the pail to fall off her head, spilling all her fresh milk. So she ended up without any milk, butter, eggs, or chickens at all.

The moral of the story was "Don't count your chickens before they hatch."

Annika remembered the story because it had math in it. And now she was counting her own chickens before they hatched. Instead of counting her chickens, she should be working hard to win them.

So she turned the page in her sudoku book and started in on the next puzzle.

4

Annika, Kelsey, and Izzy decided to bake their first batch of cookies for the carnival after school on Wednesday at Kelsey's house. They could put the cookies in the freezer so they'd stay nice and fresh till the weekend.

They stopped at the grocery store with Kelsey's mother on the way home from school to buy brown sugar, butter, eggs, and three bags of chocolate chips, enough for three batches of cookies, if they baked a batch every day between now and Saturday. They already had the rest of the ingredients in the pantry in

Kelsey's kitchen, things like flour, white sugar, and baking soda.

Annika studied the recipe on the back of the bag of chocolate chips as they waited in line to pay. "It says each batch makes five dozen cookies, so that's sixty cookies each time, so if we bake three batches, that's one hundred eighty cookies total!" Their class booth would make tons of money on chocolate chip cookies alone.

"Do you need help baking?" Mrs. Green asked once they were home with the groceries unpacked on the kitchen table.

"No!" the three girls answered.

Mr. Boone hadn't said, "I want your *parents* to get busy baking those cookies." He had said, "I want *you* to get busy baking those cookies."

"All right, but don't use the electric mixer, and call me when you're ready to put the cookies in the oven to bake. I have to supervise that part."

Kelsey's mother preheated the oven and

headed upstairs, leaving the girls to mix the dough on their own.

Kelsey found three aprons in a kitchen drawer. The aprons had flowers and teapots and kittens on them, not numerals.

Neither Annika nor Izzy had ever baked cookies before, so Kelsey took the lead.

"First we have to measure out the ingredients," she said importantly.

Annika loved measuring things. Together the girls measured two and a quarter cups of flour, Kelsey showing Annika and Izzy how to level off the top of each measuring cup with the side of a table knife so that the measurement would be exact. Kelsey then showed them how to measure three quarters of a cup of brown sugar by packing the brown sugar down firmly into the measuring cup until it reached the three-quarters line. White sugar didn't have to be packed down; it didn't smush together the way brown sugar did. One cup of butter was the same as sixteen tablespoons of butter, which was the same as two sticks of butter.

It was all new and fascinating to Annika. She had never known that baking had so much math in it—so much tasty math!

She checked the recipe again, sending Kelsey to the pantry to find baking soda, vanilla, and salt.

"I can't find the baking soda," Kelsey said, "but here are the vanilla and salt."

"Your mother said you have some," Annika said.

"Well, I can't find it."

Izzy squeezed into the pantry next to Kelsey to see if she could spot the baking soda. Izzy was good at finding things that the others couldn't find, like Kelsey's spelling homework or the ribbon that had slipped off one of Annika's long braids.

"Nope," Izzy confirmed. "I can't find baking soda anywhere."

Kelsey looked over Annika's shoulder at the recipe. "Well, it only says one teaspoon of baking soda. That's hardly anything compared to two and a quarter cups of flour. It can't matter all that much if we leave out one little teaspoon of something."

That didn't sound like a good idea to Annika. Wasn't baking like a math problem, where all the different ingredients had to add up to make the finished cookies? But Kelsey was the one who knew about baking, and if Kelsey said one teaspoon either way didn't matter, Kelsey must be right.

It was hard work using a big wooden spoon to cream together the butter and two kinds of sugar. The girls took turns blending the butter and sugars into a creamy mass. Izzy finished up because she had stronger arm muscles than the others.

"Who wants to break the first egg?" Kelsey asked.

"I do!" Izzy volunteered.

Izzy picked up the egg.

"Goodbye, egg!"

She smashed it against the side of the mixing bowl. The shell shattered, spattering egg everywhere except for into the bowl where it was supposed to go.

"Oops," Izzy said. "Someone else better do this."

Annika took a try. When she broke her egg, part of the egg white fell outside the bowl and dribbled onto the counter. When she broke the second egg, part of the eggshell fell into the bowl. She fished it out as best she could. She was definitely better at decimals and sudoku than she was at egg breaking.

The girls mixed in the eggs and vanilla, then slowly added the flour and salt, and finally dumped in the chocolate chips from the first package—or, rather, the chocolate chips that were left after Izzy's constant sampling.

"A few chocolate chips more or less won't matter," Izzy said when Kelsey scolded her. "Just like the baking soda."

Next, the girls spooned the dough onto five cookie sheets, carefully spacing the dough balls two inches apart.

"Why do they have to be two inches apart?" Izzy asked, eating a gob of dough with her fingers even though you weren't supposed to eat raw cookie dough because it had raw eggs in it.

"They spread when they're baked," Kelsey explained. "They spread, and puff up, and turn golden brown and dee-licious."

Kelsey's mother was summoned to help them put the first pan of cookies in the oven, setting the timer for nine minutes.

While they waited for the cookies to bake, Annika told them how she was trying to train Prime to do math problems.

"Poor Prime!" Izzy moaned. "Why don't you

train him to run races? I could take him on a leash with me when I go out running."

"Poor Prime," Kelsey agreed. "I think he'd like it better if you read to him. There are tons of books about dogs, millions of them."

Izzy and Kelsey would never understand! Annika gave up and changed the subject. "Do you think Mr. Boone will wear a bathing suit for his dunking at the carnival, or do you think he'll be dunked in regular clothes?"

The girls debated that question—Izzy said bathing suit, Kelsey said regular clothes—until the timer dinged.

Kelsey's mom pulled the tray out of the oven to check the cookies. They looked strangely flat, spread out a bit from the heat of the oven, but not at all plumped up as Kelsey had said they would be.

Mrs. Green frowned. "Let's give them a couple more minutes."

But after two more minutes, the cookies had

turned browner—more of a dark brown than a golden brown—but they remained as flat as before.

"Maybe they'll still taste good," Kelsey said doubtfully.

"But who will want to buy them if they look weird?" Izzy asked.

Izzy had a good point.

"There must have been something wrong with the baking soda," Kelsey's mother said.

The three girls exchanged glances.

"You did remember to put in the baking soda, didn't you?" Mrs. Green asked. "A teaspoon of baking soda?"

"We couldn't find it," Kelsey confessed. "And I figured one teaspoon of anything couldn't make all that much of a difference . . ." Her voice trailed off.

"Baking soda," Kelsey's mother said, "is what makes cookies rise."

"Oh," all three girls said together.

Mrs. Green motioned to them to follow her into the pantry.

"Here it is," she said, pulling out the baking soda box to show them. "It was right behind this big container of salt. Next time, if you can't find something, come and ask!"

Annika couldn't help being a tiny bit pleased to find out that math did matter in baking after all. But it was too late now to add baking soda to the remaining cookies already spooned out onto the other baking sheets, waiting for their turn in the oven. And it was too late to make another batch of dough today.

Annika took a nibble of one of the strange-looking cookies. It had a strange metallic taste, too—not the way a cookie should taste at all. These were cookies that even Prime wouldn't have wanted to eat.

5

On Thursday at lunch recess, as Annika opened her puzzle book, Kelsey said, "Don't you ever do anything but sudoku puzzles anymore?"

Izzy, who hadn't dashed off yet for her pickup basketball game, pointed across the playground to Simon. "Simon is obsessed with sudoku puzzles, too."

Maybe they'd figure it out. Kelsey loved reading mysteries, and now she had two clues. *Clue number one: Annika is doing sudoku puzzles all the time. Clue number two: Simon is doing sudoku puzzles all the time. Could it be that they're both competing in a sudoku contest?*

"The two of you have sudoku-itis," Kelsey said.

Izzy laughed at the funny word.

Should Annika go ahead and tell them? It was getting awfully lonely practicing all by herself. But what if they said, "A sudoku contest? Borrr-ing!"? What if they said, "Sudoku contests are dumb"?

Maybe Annika wasn't being fair to her friends.

"I was going to keep it a secret," Annika said slowly. "I was going to make it a surprise, but . . ."

Kelsey and Izzy leaned in closer.

"There's a sudoku contest at the public library this week. And I'm going to enter it on Saturday."

"And Simon is, too!" Kelsey said. So she had solved at least part of the mystery.

"Poor Simon!" Izzy said.

"He doesn't have a chance," Kelsey agreed.

Annika was glad Izzy had said "Poor Simon" instead of "Poor Annika." They had pitied "Poor Prime" for having to learn to count to three, which was hardly any counting at all. They might have pitied her for having to do something as boring and dumb as sudoku. Instead, Izzy jumped up from her seat on the bench next to Annika and began jogging in place, as if she had too much happy energy now to sit still. Kelsey's eyes were bright with excitement.

"We can time you!" Kelsey offered. "After school today at my house, in between baking cookies for the carnival, you can do a hundred puzzles, and Izzy and I will take turns timing you to see if you can go faster and faster."

"I'll be late because I have Fitness Club," Izzy put in. Twice a week all spring Izzy went to the Franklin School Fitness Club to train for the 10K race she was going to be running later that month. Now she sounded disappointed that she had to be off training for her own race instead of helping Annika train for hers. "Kelsey can time you for both of us. But don't start baking until I get there!"

"We can make up a math cheer," Kelsey suggested. She held up her hand to signal the others to be quiet while she thought.

"Okay, I have it. Annika, Annika, Annika—who? Annika, Queen of Su-do-*ku*!"

Izzy squinched up her nose. "Su-do-*ku* sounds silly."

Kelsey held up her hand again. She closed her eyes as if she were entering a trance. A moment later she opened them.

"Simon, Simon, take a bath," she chanted. "Annika is the Queen of Math."

"Take a *bath*?" Izzy asked.

"Getting dunked," Kelsey explained. "Like Mr. Boone at the carnival? Okay, I'll try again."

This time Kelsey not only closed her eyes, she sat cross-legged on the bench, holding out her hands, thumb and fingers lightly touching, as if she were meditating. When she opened her eyes, her face was serene.

"This is perfect, Miss Izzy Barr, and you can't say it isn't. Are you ready to hear it? Both of you?"

Annika and Izzy nodded.

"Annika Riz, Math Whiz."

Izzy squealed with pleasure and hugged Kelsey. Then both girls hugged Annika.

"There is no way that Simon Ellis-Smellis can beat Annika Riz, Math Whiz," Kelsey said.

Then Izzy ran off to shoot baskets, and Kelsey opened her library book.

Annika sat smiling for a long moment before starting her next sudoku puzzle, even though Simon Ellis-Smellis, over on the far bench, was still busy practicing.

She had the best friends ever.

How could she not win the sudoku contest with friends like these urging her on with her own special cheer?

Kelsey might be the best reader in the class, and the best cheer-maker-upper, but one thing she was terrible at was using Annika's stop-watch. After three attempts, Annika gave up trying to explain it to her. And while Annika sat at Kelsey's kitchen table working on a new puzzle, Kelsey leaned over her shoulder making unhelpful comments like "Could a three maybe go here?" and "I don't see why a four went *there*."

"Kelsey!" Annika waved her away.

"I'm just trying to help," Kelsey protested.

"Why don't I time myself," Annika asked, "while you read a library book?"

Preferably a nice long library book.

"But how is that helping you?" Kelsey wanted to know.

"It's—well, you made up the cheer," Annika reminded her.

"I could make up another one," Kelsey offered. She scrunched her eyes shut and furrowed her brow.

"Annika, Annika, Anni-*KAH*. She's the best, hoorah—"

"Hoorah," Annika finished the cheer for her.

Really, Prime was more helpful than Kelsey. His paws were too clumsy to operate a stopwatch, but at least he didn't talk all the time—or, worse, cheer all the time—while someone else was trying to get ready for a sudoku contest. Maybe some activities weren't meant to be done to cheers.

Izzy arrived an hour later, sweaty and panting from her run.

"I can take a turn timing you," she said after gulping down a tall glass of water.

"Um, I think I'm all right," Annika said. "Thanks, though."

Her head ached from sudoku. Numbers were exploding in her brain like hot kernels of popping corn at a carnival booth.

Speaking of carnival booths . . .

"Now that Izzy's here, we need to bake another batch of cookies," Annika reminded them.

In an instant, all three girls were wearing aprons and pulling ingredients from the fridge and pantry.

This time Annika made sure to add a teaspoon of baking soda right away to the bowl with the measured cups of flour, while Kelsey headed upstairs to enlist her mother's help with the oven and Izzy poured herself a third glass of water. Then Annika wandered over to the window to look at the dog next door playing fetch. The dog was nowhere near as cute as Prime, and Annika doubted that he could count at all.

She rejoined the others to help spoon the dough onto the baking sheets and watch as Kelsey's mom slid the first sheet into the oven.

But when the timer rang, the cookies were no longer neat round blobs. They had turned into one big mass of puffy dough, run together and spreading in every direction right up to the edges of the pan. They had become monster cookies—or, rather, one great big rectangular monster cookie.

"So who put in the baking soda?" Kelsey's mother asked.

All three girls spoke at once.

"I did," Annika said.

"I did," Kelsey said.

"I did," Izzy said.

"Girls . . ." Kelsey's mother began, but there was no point in saying anything else.

The cookies were ruined.

Again.

6

All right, Prime," Annika said when she and her father got home from Kelsey's house. "Here is why you need to learn how to count. With *one* teaspoon of baking soda, you get dozens of delicious cookies to sell at a carnival booth. With *three* teaspoons of baking soda, you get no delicious cookies at all."

Prime wagged his tail. At least he always acted enthusiastic about his math lessons, even if he hadn't learned much counting yet—or *any* counting, if Annika was going to be completely honest about it.

"I think we're not going to have you count by barking," Annika told him. "Barking hasn't worked out so well because you get too excited about counting and then you bark just because you're excited. Instead, you're going to count by tapping your paw."

Annika picked up Prime's paw to show him how it was done.

"When you see one biscuit, you give one tap."

She tapped his paw in place.

"When you see two biscuits, you give two taps."

She did it for him. Tap. Tap.

"Oh, and we're going to work up later to counting to three. For now we're just going to try counting to one and two."

From the bag in the pantry she retrieved a dog biscuit.

"Sit!"

Prime jumped up to try to get the biscuit.

"Prime, how can you possibly tap your paw the right number of times if you're using it to leap up into the air?"

With her non-biscuit-holding hand, she pushed Prime's hind end down until he was sort of sitting.

"One biscuit!"

She held it up.

Prime barked and barked and barked.

"Now you tap your foot once."

When she bent down to help him with the tapping, Prime snatched the biscuit out of her hand.

"Prime!" Annika wailed.

Dog biscuits were too distracting, that was the trouble. Somebody should invent a new kind of treat that dogs liked enough to do tricks for, but didn't like so much that they were too excited about the treat to do any tricks at all.

Annika finished the lesson by tapping

Prime's foot once more while she said "One," and twice more while she said "Two." She didn't reward him for it afterward. He had eaten his reward already.

At school Friday morning, Annika, Kelsey, and Izzy met by the big stuffed elephant in the front hallway. Perched on its trunk was a sign that said, WIN ME AT THE CARNIVAL THIS SATURDAY! Seated, the elephant was taller than Annika and twice as wide.

"I hope I win you," Izzy told the elephant.

"I hope I win you, too," Kelsey echoed. "If one of the three of us wins, we can all share him, don't you think?"

"Are you kidding? I'm not buying a ticket," Annika said, shocked that the others were ignoring the plain math facts of the situation. "Do you know what your chances are of winning? There are four hundred kids at Franklin School, so if each one buys a ticket, you have a one-in-four-hundred chance of winning. That's practically no chance at all."

"But somebody has to win," Izzy pointed out.

"So it could be us," Kelsey said.

"Forget it," Annika told them. "You have a better chance of . . . of . . ." She tried to think of something completely preposterous. "Of getting Mrs. Molina to agree to be dunked in the dunking booth!"

Kelsey stroked the elephant's trunk.

Izzy stood on tiptoe to pat him on his head.

Annika looked away, determined to ignore him completely.

"I know the carnival is tomorrow evening," Mrs. Molina said once the bell had rung and everyone was in his or her seat. "But we are not going to spend any class time talking about the carnival today, do you understand?"

Cody put up his hand.

"Yes, Cody?"

WIN ME
at the
CARNIVA
this
SATURD

"I heard what the really gross booth is going to be. The one Mr. Boone was talking about."

"Tell us!" lots of kids shouted.

"We are not going to spend class time talking about the carnival," Mrs. Molina repeated.

Another kid waved his hand. Without being called on, he announced, "I baked four dozen cookies last night."

"I baked five dozen," another kid reported.

Annika, Kelsey, and Izzy would have had ten dozen cookies by now, if they hadn't put too little baking soda in the first batch and too much in the second batch. But instead they had ended up with no sellable cookies at all.

"Open your math books to page 192," Mrs. Molina said.

Nobody did, except for Simon and Annika.

"I want to win the elephant!"

"My mom is helping my brother's class with face painting!"

"Mr. Boone is going to get soaked!"

"The two other third-grade teachers are going to get dunked, too!"

Mrs. Molina looked as angry as Annika had ever seen her.

"If you don't settle down . . ." Mrs. Molina began. She paused, obviously trying to think of a suitably terrible threat. Annika knew she wished she had the power to threaten to cancel the entire carnival there and then. "If you don't settle down, I'll give you a decimal quiz."

It must have been enough of a threat because the students finally opened their books, though Izzy was still giggling.

"Izzy Barr, why don't you start us off with question number four?" Mrs. Molina asked.

Izzy's giggles died away.

"Question number four," she said, clearly stalling for time.

"Yes, question four. What fraction is point one?"

Izzy hesitated.

How could anybody not know the answer to such an easy one? Annika wasn't going to whisper the answer to her this time, she wasn't!

But then she thought of how Izzy had come running back to Kelsey's house to time her sudoku practice. And how Izzy had joined in Kelsey's cheer. And how much both of her friends wanted her to win the contest.

"One-tenth," she whispered.

"One-tenth," Izzy repeated.

The next kid called on got her answer wrong, and the kid after that.

"I can't wait," Mrs. Molina said crossly, "until this carnival is over!"

7

At lunch recess, Annika raced through another sudoku puzzle, politely refusing Kelsey's offer of timing help; Izzy was off playing kickball. She finished writing in the last number—ta-dah!—when she realized that someone was standing a few feet away, watching her with friendly curiosity.

It was Mr. Boone.

"You're getting remarkably good at those, Annika," he said.

Annika couldn't remember any time that Mr. Boone had ever spoken to her before, just to her, all by herself. She couldn't believe that he knew her name *and* that he had noticed she was working so hard at sudoku.

Too shy to say anything, she sat silent, feeling her cheeks flush.

Kelsey took over for her. "The public library's having a sudoku contest this week, and there's going to be a winner for each grade, and Annika's going to be the third-grade winner!"

"Well, I'm going to *try* to win," Annika corrected, grateful to find her voice again. Honesty compelled her to add, "Simon Ellis is awfully good at math. Plus, there will be kids from all the other schools, too."

"Step one is trying," Mr. Boone said, "and you're certainly doing that."

Then he smiled at both girls. "How is the cookie baking coming along?"

"Horrible!" Kelsey replied.

She told him about the two baking soda

disasters. Annika wouldn't have done that. She wanted the principal to think she was a math whiz, not a baking dummy. But he laughed his big, booming laugh, and that made Annika laugh, too.

"If step one is trying," he said, "then step two is trying again. And again. And again."

The bell rang for the end of lunch recess, and after grinning at them one more time, Mr. Boone strolled away.

After school, the three friends decided to take Mr. Boone's advice and try a third time at baking their carnival cookies.

This time Annika read aloud from the recipe, one ingredient at a time, while Kelsey and Izzy took turns doing the measuring.

"*One* teaspoon of baking soda," Annika read.

"We know that!" Kelsey said.

"One, and only one!" Izzy said.

Once again, Kelsey's mother put the cookies in the oven for them. Today they had made the cookies a little bit larger so that they had four dozen, not five dozen. They were going to bake them all at the same time, placing two of the trays side by side on the middle oven rack and two trays on the rack underneath. They needed to finish up the baking quickly because Kelsey's family was heading out to have a picnic dinner in the park while listening to her older brother play the trombone in the school band's "Musical Month of May" concert.

"It's not ideal to bake them all at once like this," Kelsey's mother lamented. "But I'm afraid we're in a bit of a rush this afternoon. Call me when the timer dings."

With the cookies safely in the oven—each cookie with the perfect amount of baking soda in it—Izzy went out for a quick run around the block a few times while Annika curled up with her sudoku book and Kelsey curled up with *Betsy and Tacy Go Downtown.*

Cozily settled on the other end of the family-room couch from Kelsey, Annika lost herself in her puzzle, working faster and harder than she had ever worked before, as fast and hard as she'd need to work when she headed off to do the actual contest—tomorrow morning!

A 7? No, there couldn't be a 7 there. It had to be an 8.

Another 8 below.

She needed to put in two more 4s.

There went one of them!

Now a 2 . . .

She sensed rather than saw Kelsey's mother rushing by them. Kelsey was still hunched over her book.

"Girls!" Mrs. Green called to them in evident distress. "Didn't you smell your cookies burning?"

Now that Mrs. Green mentioned it, Annika did smell something burning.

No, she smelled something completely burnt.

Had they both forgotten to set the timer? Or had neither girl heard its warning ding, one lost in the world of reading, the other lost in the world of math? Either way, it didn't matter now.

Mrs. Green had already grabbed the trays out of the oven. She flung open the kitchen windows to air out the room just as the smoke alarm went off with a deafening beep.

The cookies were properly shaped this time; they had risen the correct amount. But they were black like nuggets of coal mined deep from the bowels of the earth.

"Oh, girls!" Kelsey's mother moaned, once she had turned off the alarm.

"What happened?" Izzy asked, coming into the

kitchen from the back door, panting after her run.

"Don't ask!" Kelsey said.

Silently the three girls scraped the blackened lumps into the garbage.

8

When Annika woke up in her math house on Saturday morning, she lingered in bed, sandwiched between sheets with brightly colored numerals printed all over them. The sheets had all the letters of the alphabet on them, too; she suspected they were intended for little kids just learning their numbers and letters, not for big third graders who were already good readers and math whizzes. But she loved them anyway.

Maybe the red, blue, and yellow numerals on her pillow—the sheets seemed designed to teach colors, too—would seep into her brain if she lay there long enough. Then they would slide down her arm and pop out the end of her pencil when she sat down at the library in another hour to do the sudoku contest.

She didn't let herself open a sudoku book at the breakfast table. She didn't want her brain to be tired out from sudoku before the contest even began. Prime's training would have to wait as well. The dog didn't seem to mind, lying at her feet underneath the table as she sprinkled salt from the 3-shaker and pepper from the 4-shaker onto her scrambled eggs. She hoped eggs were good brain food.

"Do you feel ready for the contest?" her mother asked.

Annika nodded, her mouth full of egg. She was definitely ready! But dozens of other third graders from all over the city must be ready, too—including Simon.

"Don't feel you have to rush through the contest puzzle," her mother told her. "Calm and steady is best. And take plenty of deep breaths."

After swallowing another eggy mouthful, Annika took a few deep breaths, for practice. Maybe deep breaths would send more oxygen to her brain. She did feel more relaxed when she was done.

She looked down admiringly at her $E=mc^2$ T-shirt and imagined Einstein working calmly and steadily on the theory of relativity, taking lots of deep breaths along the way.

When she stood up from the table, Prime dashed over to the pantry door, obviously expecting her to produce dog biscuits for another counting lesson. He clearly was a very smart dog, even if he couldn't yet count to two, or even to one, for that matter.

"Not now, Prime," she told him.

Then she relented.

"Okay, one very quick lesson."

She reminded him to tap his paw once for

one biscuit, twice for two, demonstrating again how to tap, in case he had forgotten.

"Now you do it," she told him. "All by yourself."

She held up one of the biscuits she had retrieved from the pantry. "One!" she said loudly and distinctly.

Prime didn't tap his foot, but he did give one low, deep bark. Maybe barking was going to work out better than paw tapping after all.

"Excellent, Prime!"

Annika gave him the biscuit.

She held up two biscuits, one in each hand, so he could see them clearly. "Two!"

Prime barked seven times.

Oh, well. At least he had given one bark for one biscuit. And he had gotten the idea that two was a bigger number than one. That was something. Still, she had to admit that her star pupil—her only pupil—wasn't yet ready to win a counting contest. Or even to enter one.

* * *

Annika's father drove her to the library. She wanted to get there right when it opened at nine. In her hand she clutched three perfectly sharpened pencils with three never-before-used erasers.

"I'll be back in an hour or so to pick you up," her father said as he gave her a parting kiss. "Good luck, sweetie."

But Annika knew there was no luck involved in sudoku, nothing except whatever talent you started out with, plus lots and lots of practice.

She had somehow expected to see Simon there, already waiting on the library steps, but she was the only one hurrying through the library doors on the dot of nine. It probably would have been too much of a coincidence if she and Simon had both arrived at the exact same time. Simon could have done the contest any day during the past week, and there was still the rest of the day until the library closed at five o'clock, right when the Franklin School carnival was going to begin.

Annika shivered with happiness at the thought of having a sudoku contest and an all-school carnival both on the same day. If only one of their batches of cookies had turned out! She hated to think how disappointed Mr. Boone would be if he knew. If he was willing to be dunked over and over again, the least Annika and her friends could do was bake some cookies to sell.

But she couldn't think about that now.

She found the children's librarian at her desk, a grandmotherly woman who looked up at Annika with a friendly smile.

"I'm here for the contest," Annika said.

The librarian looked puzzled.

"The sudoku contest?" Annika explained.

"Oh, the sudoku contest! Let me see, I have the contest materials around here somewhere. What grade are you in?"

"Third." Annika drew herself up taller and straighter.

"All right, here it is. I see you came prepared with your own pencils. Now where should I put you?"

This librarian must be a special Saturday librarian. She certainly didn't seem to know anything about what had been going on in the library all week, with kids from all over the city streaming in to compete in the contest.

"How about the quiet study room?" The librarian led Annika to a small room off the main children's area, containing one rectangular table surrounded by six chairs.

The librarian consulted the directions for the contest on the sheet she held in her hand. "When you're ready, I'll record the time you begin"—she pointed to the digital clock sitting on one end of the table that read 9:06—"and when you're all done, write down the time you finish and then bring the completed puzzle to me. All right?"

Annika swallowed hard. This was it!

She was glad no one else had shown up to do the contest at the same time. It would have made her nervous to hear every scritch and scratch of someone else's pencil, especially if that someone was Simon.

"Okay," she said.

"Take a deep breath," the librarian said kindly, just like Annika's mother.

"And good luck!" she said, just like Annika's father.

"Ready, set . . ." She paused to write 9:07 on the top of Annika's paper. "Go!"

Annika forced herself to take a deep breath. Then she leaped into action.

$E=mc^2$

4.

Another 4.

6.

2.

1.

1.

6.

She didn't let herself glance at the clock, refusing to waste a precious second that could be given to entering numbers on the page. What if Simon came bursting through the door right now, interrupting her train of thought? *No, don't think about that! Keep working!*

4.

2.

She was stuck. She couldn't see what number to put in next.

Wait. No. Yes. 3!

Another minute—it felt like a whole minute—spent just thinking and not writing anything at all.

Then a 4. Another 4. And the final 6.

Done!

Half-afraid, she looked at the clock. 9:21! Fourteen minutes! Her best time yet!

But was it better than Simon's best time?

Was it better than everyone else's best time?

Back at the librarian's desk, she held out the completed puzzle and waited to see what the librarian would have to say.

"That was fast!" The librarian gave her a warm smile. But maybe she smiled that way at all the contestants.

Annika wished she dared ask her, *Faster than this boy in my class, about my height, kind of skinny, with pencils sticking out of his pocket?*

Instead she said, "When will we find out who wins?"

She meant, *When will I find out if I win?*

"I'm so glad you asked!" the librarian said. "I

almost forgot to have you fill out this entry form with your name, phone number, the name of your school, and your teacher's name. We'll call the winners as soon as we have the results."

Annika finished filling out the form just as her father appeared to collect her.

"How did it go?" he asked her once they were in the car.

"Pretty good," Annika said. "I got my best time ever. But it all depends on how fast Simon did. I don't want to count my chickens before they hatch."

"Whatever happens," her father said, "your mother and I think we hatched one very smart chicken, and we're both proud of you just for trying."

9

How was it?" Kelsey and Izzy shrieked as they burst into Annika's house that afternoon, dropped off by Izzy's dad.

Annika gave them two thumbs-up. Prime joined in with a series of triumphant barks.

"I had my best time ever, but Simon might have done even better. Lots of kids might have beat me. So I don't really know anything yet."

"Nobody is better in math than you are," Izzy said.

"If you didn't give us the answers in math class, we'd die!" Kelsey said.

Annika was glad to hear their praise, but part of her wanted to say: *If I didn't give you the answers in math class, you might actually learn some math yourself. And then you'd do as well on tests as you do in class. And maybe you'd start to think math is cool and fun. Which it is!*

But she didn't. Instead she said, "Do you want to see how Prime can count to one?"

"Are you still making him do that?" Kelsey demanded. "It's . . . it's . . . cruelty to animals!"

Izzy chimed in. "It's probably against the law."

"He likes doing it." Annika reached down to pet him. "Don't you, Prime?"

He wagged his tail as if to say *Yes, indeed I do.*

As the others watched, Annika had Prime bark once for one biscuit. He did it! But then he barked once for two biscuits, and on the next try, he barked five times.

"But he still barked once for one biscuit," Annika pointed out proudly.

Kelsey and Izzy petted him luxuriously, maybe to make up to him for having to submit to a math lesson. Prime rolled over on his back so that they could rub his tummy, now comfortably filled with doggie biscuits. Kelsey had insisted on giving him five biscuits for his five barks, and Izzy had already given him two biscuits for his two barks. But there was no limit to the number of dog biscuits Prime was eager to eat.

"Four more hours until the carnival," Izzy said, once everyone was tired of dog petting.

Annika couldn't wait to see all the booths, especially Mr. Boone's dunking tank, but she hated to think of everyone else arriving with dozens of home-baked cookies while the three of them arrived with nothing. Zip. Nada. Zero! The famous number invented in India hundreds and hundreds of years ago that represented the absence of anything at all.

"I wish we had something to sell at the carnival," she said.

"Should we try baking one more batch of cookies?" Kelsey asked halfheartedly.

"No!" Izzy said. "Three strikes and we're out." In addition to training for her 10K race, Izzy was on a girls' softball team.

Annika knew "Three strikes and you're out" was the rule in softball. But it wasn't necessarily a good rule for life. In life you might have to try more than three times to get what you wanted. Look how many times she had already tried to train Prime to count! Still, she thought Izzy was right that, given their track record, baking a fourth batch of chocolate chip cookies wasn't a good idea.

"We could sell something else," she said. "Something that goes with cookies, like—"

"Lemonade!" Izzy and Kelsey shouted together.

"Like lemonade!" Annika said.

* * *

The girls looked up a recipe on the Internet for extra-fancy, old-fashioned, fresh-squeezed lemonade, like the kind you could buy at the baseball games downtown in the summer. In Annika's kitchen cupboards they found most of the things they'd need: a five-pound bag of sugar, a big stack of plastic cups, a box of straws, and a juice squeezer. Kelsey called her mother to ask if she'd be willing to help make the lemonade at the booth, and Annika's mother agreed to drive them to the store to buy ice and lemons.

"But I want you girls to contribute some of the money to buy the lemons," Mrs. Riz told them. "Maybe you would have been more careful with the baking if you had bought the ingredients yourselves."

That wasn't true. Even if they had spent a thousand dollars on chocolate chips—not that

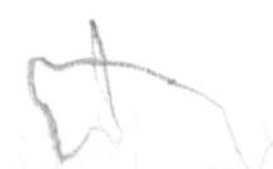

they had a thousand dollars to spend—none of them would have heard the timer ding.

With money fished out of Kelsey's and Izzy's pockets and Annika's piggy bank, the girls bought six dozen lemons, three for a dollar, and an enormous bag of crushed ice for five dollars. The total came to almost thirty dollars, but Annika's mother relented and paid for half of it.

Back at Annika's house, as the three girls admired their lemons, laid out on Annika's number-patterned tablecloth, Annika couldn't shake the feeling that something was wrong.

Maybe she was jumpy waiting for the contest results. Or maybe they had forgotten some important item for the lemonade. Sugar, lemons, cups, straws, juice squeezer, water, ice—what else could there be? They'd need measuring spoons, a sharp knife, and a cutting board for cutting the lemons, but her mother was going to send those along to the carnival so that Kelsey's mother, helping at the booth, could cut the lemons on the spot. They needed a sign, but Kelsey could add the lemonade price to the sign she had already volunteered to make for the cookies. Kelsey had beautiful printing and loved making signs.

Still, something didn't feel right in Annika's math house.

Then she realized. Prime hadn't greeted them at the door, jumping up to lick their faces and giving his frantic happy barks. He hadn't come dashing into the kitchen, skidding on the tile floor with his clumsy paws.

Where was Prime?

"Have you seen Prime anywhere?" Annika asked her father, who had arrived in the kitchen to take a break from grading math papers.

"Can't say that I have. But he has to be somewhere in the house. There's no way he could have gotten outside while you were gone."

But he looked more worried than he sounded.

E=mc²

Prime never failed to welcome them when they came home.

"Prime!" Annika called. "Prime!"

She heard one feeble answering bark.

"Prime!"

Annika listened harder this time. A second muffled bark came from the pantry. She must have forgotten to shut the pantry door all the way when she hurried off on the lemonade shopping trip.

There, on the floor of the narrow pantry, lay Prime.

Beside him lay what had once been a partially full bag of dog biscuits, but was now a completely empty bag.

Prime looked up at Annika with guilty eyes, gave one low moan, and threw up.

"Dad!" Annika yelled. "Mom!"

Behind her, Kelsey and Izzy gaped at Prime, while Annika's dad grabbed a mop from the mudroom and her mother arrived with an armful of old towels.

"Oh, Prime!" Annika scolded him, but it was really her fault for leaving the pantry door ajar. And for getting him so interested in dog biscuits in the first place.

His stomach empty, Prime apparently felt better. He barked and barked and barked and barked, more than Annika had ever heard him bark before, as if he was barking once for every dog biscuit in the entire bag.

"See?" Annika said to Kelsey and Izzy, half laughing, half crying. "Prime did learn how to count after all."

At least he now knew the difference between a few dog biscuits and too many dog biscuits, which was what counting was all about.

And maybe that was enough math for even a mathematically minded dog to learn.

10

Annika's father was going to drive Kelsey and Izzy home at three o'clock to get ready for the carnival.

"Don't forget to make the sign," Annika told Kelsey.

"I won't," Kelsey promised.

"Let us know if you get a phone call that you won," Izzy told Annika.

"They can't call until the contest ends at five," Annika said, "and we'll be at the carnival by then."

"Well, maybe your time was so amazing that

they declared you the winner early because it was already a world record for third-grade sudoku," Izzy said.

"You guys!" Annika shoved them out the door to the garage. Then she did go check the answering machine, just in case she'd somehow missed hearing the phone ring.

The three friends were the first kids at Mrs. Molina's booth so that they could start making their lemonade. They worked together in a row.

Kelsey's mother cut the lemons.

Kelsey filled a tall plastic cup with ice and poured in one cup of water.

Izzy stirred in a heaping tablespoon of sugar.

Annika finished by squeezing in the juice of one lemon; she put half of the squeezed-out lemon in the cup, too, to look pretty.

By the time the carnival opened right at five, they had twenty-four cups of lemonade lined up ready to sell. Lots of kids had arrived with cookies as well, all of the cookies looking as if they contained the right amount of baking soda and had baked the right number of minutes.

"Where's the sign?" Annika suddenly remembered.

"It's in my mom's car," Kelsey said. "I'll go get it. Relax!"

How could Annika possibly relax when at this very minute the sudoku contest at the public library was coming to an end? Her parents were coming to the carnival later, but they had promised to listen for the phone and have one of them drive over to Franklin School the minute they heard anything.

If they heard anything, of course. The librarian hadn't said she'd call everybody; she said she'd call the winners.

Was Annika a winner or not?

She saw Simon approaching the booth, carrying a carton so enormous he could barely manage it all by himself. He began unloading plate after plate filled with cookies of every kind: chocolate chip, oatmeal raisin, cookies studded with M&Ms, cookies filled with raspberry jam, cookies frosted with icing in yellow and green, the Franklin School colors.

So Simon wasn't only a math whiz, a reading whiz, a science whiz, and a social studies whiz. Apparently he was a cookie-baking whiz, too.

Annika was dying to ask him what his sudoku contest time had been. Was it faster than hers or not? But she couldn't bear to come right out with the question. What if he had beaten her, even after all her practice? Kelsey and Izzy would be so disappointed, too, and they'd try to say something meant to be comforting, like "Cheer up, it was just a dumb math thing anyway."

"Go walk around and check out the other booths," Izzy ordered her as Annika stood twisting one of the lemonade straws so tightly that it broke. "Kelsey and I can take the first shift selling the lemonade. Go!"

Annika hurried off to explore the carnival.

She saw Cody waiting in line at one of the fourth-grade booths. This must be the super-gross one he kept talking about.

NOSE PICKING BOOTH, the sign said.

On a large plywood board was painted a big grinning face. From the two huge nostril holes cut into the painted nose flowed a stream of fake green slime. For two tickets—fifty cents—kids could reach into the nose and pull out a prize. Annika could tell that the fun wasn't getting the prize as much as it was accepting a dare to do something so disgusting.

The biggest crowd was at the dunking tank. Above a tall swimming pool Mr. Boone was sitting on a small plastic seat. He wasn't wearing his bathing suit, but he had on shorts and a Franklin School T-shirt. Annika had never seen a principal in shorts before. His bare feet dangled from his perch. She had never seen a barefoot principal before, either. As of this moment he was completely dry.

"Don't dunk me!" he pleaded to the kids swarming around the tank. "Have some respect for your distinguished principal! Please don't pay eight tickets to dunk me while raising money for the Franklin School PTA!"

But the ticket taker was already accepting a string of eight tickets—worth two dollars—from one of the pushiest fifth graders, who had shoved his way to the front of the throng.

"Don't dunk me!" Mr. Boone mock-wailed. "Don't—"

Down he went with a terrific splash to deafening applause and squeals from kids who got drenched from the spray.

After shaking himself like a wet dog, Mr.

Boone climbed back up the ladder to his perch.

"Don't dunk me again!" he called out to the crowd. "Once was enough! Don't do—"

Splash!

Then one of the second-grade teachers, also wearing shorts and a T-shirt, climbed up for her own plunge to watery doom.

Annika knew she should get back to Mrs. Molina's class booth to let Izzy and Kelsey have some carnival fun, but it was hard to leave the hilarity of the dunking booth. Plus, she wanted to get her face painted, fish for prizes, buy cotton candy—everything! But first she'd wait until Mr. Boone got dunked again.

"Annika!"

Over the catcalls from the kids by the dunking tank, she heard someone shouting her name. She whirled around to see who it could be.

Hurrying toward her was her father, the grin

DUNK

on his face as wide as infinity, a number greater than any other number.

That could mean only one thing.

"Guess who won the sudoku prize out of all the third graders in the entire city?"

Annika snuggled into his embrace. She would have had a harder time winning if she hadn't been the daughter of two math parents living in the math house with a math dog.

Then she let him head home to do a little more grading while she pelted back to the booth to share the good news with Kelsey and Izzy.

Now they'd see how cool math was!

Now they'd try to do math, too!

Mrs. Molina's booth had a gratifyingly long line of customers in front of it. Five or six students were helping with the sales, as well as parent helpers and Mrs. Molina, too. Their teacher wasn't wearing shorts and a Franklin

School T-shirt; even at a carnival she was wearing the same teacher clothes she wore every day to school.

Izzy was busy handing a gray-haired woman customer a cup of lemonade, while Kelsey was handing her one of Simon's cookies.

Annika couldn't wait another second to tell them. She wouldn't have blurted out the news in front of Simon, not wanting to make him feel bad in the middle of the carnival, but he wasn't at the booth right now.

"I won!" she called out.

"Yay!" shouted Izzy.

"Hooray!" shouted Kelsey.

Then Annika recognized the woman taking the first sip of her lemonade. It was the children's librarian!

"I see you heard the good news," she said, smiling. "Your father told me he'd get the message to you right away. Congratulations!"

Annika beamed.

With the librarian standing right here, she had to take advantage of the chance to ask the thing she wanted to know most. “How many third graders entered the contest?”

It was wonderful enough to have beaten Simon, but every third-grade class in every school probably had its own Simon, and it was even more wonderful to think of beating them all.

“Well,” the librarian said, looking uncomfortable, “I know we didn’t send out publicity to the schools soon enough. It’s a busy time of year for a lot of people.”

“So how many were there?” Annika persisted.

Even beating six people would be something to be proud of.

Even beating one person, if that person was Simon Ellis.

"Well," the librarian said again, unable to meet Annika's eyes. "The fact of the matter is . . ."

Annika waited for her to finish the sentence.

"You were the only one."

11

Annika's cheeks flamed.

No one else had entered the contest?

Not even Simon?

All that practice to get her time down to fourteen minutes, when she could have won with a time of fourteen *hours*, because apparently she was the only third grader in the entire city who cared enough about anything math-y to enter the contest.

She waited to hear Kelsey and Izzy howling with laughter.

We told you that everybody else thinks math is boring!

But they didn't laugh even a little bit.

"I bet Simon was afraid to enter!" Izzy said.

"He knew you'd beat him, so he didn't even try!" Kelsey chimed in.

They were the best friends anyone could ever have, even if they thought she was weird for loving math. She gulped back the sob that was surging up in her throat.

The grownup in line behind the librarian interrupted their conversation. "Are you girls here to gab or to sell cookies and lemonade?"

The librarian shot him a silencing look. "Congratulations again, Annika. You deserve to win not just for being such an amazing sudoku-puzzle-solver, but for being the only kid who even tried."

Annika forced herself to give a small smile. Mr. Boone had said something just like that the other day, and her dad had said something like that, too. Maybe, in the end, the important thing was just trying.

"So what do I owe you for the cookie and lemonade?" the librarian asked. She looked at the sign Kelsey had made. "Oh, I see, one ticket for the lemonade and one for the cookie."

As Izzy took the two tickets, for the first time Annika saw Kelsey's sign, lettered in Kelsey's neat, colorful printing:

DELICIOUS HOME-BAKED COOKIES!

1 ticket per cookie!

DELICIOUS FRESH-SQUEEZED LEMONADE!

1 ticket per glass!

Oh, no!

Annika should have talked to Kelsey first, before she made the sign!

The most important thing about a sign for a carnival sale wasn't what it looked like, but what price it said.

She tugged on Kelsey's sleeve and drew her

away from the booth. Looking bewildered, Izzy followed. They deserved a break anyway; Simon had showed up to take his shift.

"One ticket per glass?" Annika demanded, trying to keep her voice level.

Even Prime would know better than that!

"It's the same price as the cookies," Kelsey said defensively.

"People have been buying a lot of it," Izzy backed her up.

"Do the math!" Annika wailed.

Her two friends stared at her. They had never done a math problem voluntarily in their lives. She would have to help them through this one.

"How much is a ticket worth?" she asked.

"Twenty-five cents," both girls replied.

"And each cup is made with the juice of one lemon," she continued.

They nodded.

"How much did each lemon cost?"

Kelsey and Izzy both shrugged.

"I don't remember," Kelsey admitted.

"It added up to a lot of money, I know that much," Izzy said.

"Exactly! It added up to a lot of money, because we bought six dozen lemons, and they were three for a dollar!"

Amazingly, both girls still didn't seem to get it.

"Three for a dollar," Annika repeated. "So how much did each lemon cost? And, no, I'm not going to tell you the answer this time! And I'm not going to tell you any answers anymore, ever again. I'll help you learn math, but I won't do math for you. I've been whispering math answers to you all year long, and look what happens: you can't even tell me how much a lemon costs!"

Now Kelsey and Izzy had the same panicked, paralyzed expression, as if Mrs. Molina had just asked them to do a decimal problem. Actually, this was about to turn into a real-life decimal problem.

Mrs. Molina had drawn closer, apparently interested to hear what the three friends were arguing about. Annika could just imagine a small smile playing around the corners of the teacher's mouth.

Izzy and Kelsey conferred with each other in low voices.

Then Izzy said, "Well, if lemons are three for a dollar, then each one costs a third of a dollar."

"But what's a third of a dollar?" Kelsey had always been even worse at math than Izzy. "Okay, a quarter of a dollar is a quarter—it's twenty-five cents. So a third of a dollar has to be more than that."

"Thirty-three cents!" Izzy suddenly shouted.

"Thirty-three and a third cents," Annika corrected. "But you can round it down to thirty-three."

DELICIOUS
HOME-BAKED
COOKIES!
1 ticket per cookie!

She heard Mrs. Molina give a low chuckle of satisfaction.

"Oh," Kelsey said then, her face crumpling. "The price is too low! If each lemon cost thirty-three cents, and we're selling the lemonade for a quarter a glass, then we're selling it for way less than it cost to make it!"

Even energetic, perky Izzy looked close to tears. "I've been squeezing those stupid lemons forever, and we're making hardly any money? First we ruined all those horrible cookies, and now even our genius lemonade idea is a total bust. Maybe the three of us should just give up."

"Quit while we're ahead," Kelsey agreed.

"No, quit while we're *behind*!" Izzy said. "Before we get even *further* behind!"

Annika felt sorry for them, now that the sad mathematical truth of the situation had finally dawned.

"Look," she said. "All we have to do is change the price. It's still pretty early in the evening, so we can sell lots more glasses at the correct price, which should be . . ."

She thought for a moment. She didn't know what the sugar, cups, and straws had cost, but it probably wasn't that much, and the ice hadn't been too expensive, either. Two tickets—fifty cents—would cover the cost of all the ingredients and materials, but if that's all they made, they might as well have just donated the money and skipped all the work of making the lemonade.

"Three tickets," she concluded. "Does anyone have a marker?"

"I have one here in my purse," Mrs. Molina offered.

Kelsey and Izzy accepted it gratefully. Kelsey used her beautiful printing to turn "1 ticket" into "3 tickets," so that it didn't even look like a correction, but as if that had been the original price.

Hooray for math!

"We're running low on lemonade," one of the parent helpers called out.

"I'll take over," Annika told her friends. "Go and have fun at the carnival."

Kelsey and Izzy ran off to the dunking tank while Annika joined Simon in the lemonade assembly line. As they worked together squeezing lemons and measuring sugar and water, she waited to see if Simon would say anything about why he hadn't entered the contest.

He didn't. So she finally said, not as a question, really, just as a comment, "You didn't enter the sudoku contest."

"I know," he said glumly. "I should have done it after school during the week, but I waited until today, and then I got busy with baking a gazillion cookies for the carnival with my mom, and when I looked at the clock, it was too late. So I blew it. Did you do it?"

Annika nodded. She might as well tell him. "I just found out that I won."

She didn't need to add that she was the only kid who had even entered the contest. Winning was still winning.

"That's cool!" Simon said. "I probably wouldn't have won anyway. My best time wasn't all that great."

Annika sucked in her breath. Should she ask? Or was it better not to know? No, she had to ask. "What *was* your best time?"

"Around sixteen minutes. How about you?"

All her happiness came rushing back, but she tried to sound modest. "Fourteen."

So even if Simon had entered, she probably would have won!

Cody Harmon was supposed to be starting his shift, replacing Simon, but he wasn't there yet. When he finally raced up, he was panting with excitement.

"Mrs. Molina," he called out, "I just checked,

and any other teachers who want to be dunked can still do it!"

Mrs. Molina's face showed no eagerness for dunking.

"Come on, Mrs. Molina," Cody begged. "You'll do it, won't you? Mr. Boone was already dunked thirty-seven times!"

All the kids working at the booth fell silent, obviously waiting to see what Mrs. Molina would say. But none of them joined in with Cody's pleading.

How could Mrs. Molina be dunked in her regular teacher clothes?

How could she be dunked while wearing her regular teacher glasses?

How could she be dunked and still be Mrs. Molina?

Mrs. Molina was stern and cross sometimes during math class, but she loved math the way that Annika did, and she had been the one to tell Annika about the sudoku contest.

Annika wanted her still to be Mrs. Molina.

With Cody's entreating eyes upon her, Mrs. Molina adjusted her glasses.

"Boys and girls," she said, "Mr. Boone and I show our school spirit in different ways, just as all of you show your spirit in different ways. Annika showed her spirit today by representing our class in a citywide sudoku contest. She's just been named the third-grade winner for the entire district."

So Mrs. Molina had overheard that conversation as well.

"Mr. Boone clearly enjoys being dunked in a dunking tank," she went on. "I do not. Different people enjoy different things. And we can all contribute to our school in different ways. Here's how I plan to contribute: whatever cookies we have left over at the end of the evening, I will purchase myself to donate to the senior citizen center downtown."

The kids clapped for Mrs. Molina then. Cody looked disappointed, but Annika knew her other classmates also seemed relieved that Mrs. Molina would still be Mrs. Molina, with dry clothes and neatly combed hair.

Besides, Mrs. Molina was right.

People were different.

Not everybody loved being dunked in a dunking tank and thought it was the most fun ever.

Not everybody loved math and thought it was the coolest subject ever.

But everybody should at least pay enough attention in math to be able to know how to price a glass of lemonade!

Two hours later, Annika, Kelsey, and Izzy were together eating cotton candy and fishing for prizes at the second-grade fishpond. Annika had won a sparkly bracelet, and Izzy had won a cute clip for her hair; Kelsey was about to dip her fishing pole into the water.

Then, over the loudspeakers set up for the carnival came Mr. Boone's booming voice.

"Ladies and gentlemen, boys and girls, the carnival will come to an end in ten minutes. That's not a minute too soon for me, because I am completely soaked!"

From the carnival crowd came hearty cheers.

"Now it's time for our raffle drawing to see who wins the enormous stuffed elephant that has graced our Franklin School front hallway all week. We're doing the drawing right now over by the dunking tank."

Kelsey and Izzy took off running.

Annika didn't bother to run after them. She hadn't bothered to buy a raffle ticket, either. No true math person would buy a raffle ticket when you had such a mathematically low chance of winning.

Instead she headed back to their class booth and started counting up tickets in the ticket box to see how much money Mrs. Molina's class had made at the carnival. The box was stuffed full to overflowing.

"All right," came Mr. Boone's voice over the speakers again. "We've drawn our winning ticket. Luckily I didn't drip water all over it, so I can still read the winning name. The winner of our elephant is—"

Annika hardly listened, busy counting under her breath: forty-seven, forty-eight, forty-nine.

"Our winner is one of our terrific third graders: Annika Riz!"

Annika must have heard him wrong. Maybe some other third grader had a name that sounded like hers, if you weren't really paying attention.

Then Izzy sprinted up to her, screaming, "You won, you won, you won!"

Breathless, Kelsey raced up to her, too.

"No, I didn't! I couldn't have won," said Annika. "I didn't even buy a ticket! I would never buy a raffle ticket."

"*We* bought it!" Kelsey crowed.

"We bought three tickets, one for each of us," Izzy sang out.

"I know you said raffles were dumb," Kelsey explained, "but we figured, okay, if we enter we probably won't win. But if we don't enter, if we don't at least try, we definitely won't win. And we did win!"

"We can share him," Annika said. "He can belong to all of us."

"Because we're best friends!" Kelsey and Izzy said together.

And the three best friends hugged again.